MERMAID ACADEMY

Cora took hold of Sparkle's back fin and felt a rush of magical energy. They flicked their tails, and the next moment they were racing through the water at double speed!

LOOK OUT FOR MORE ADVENTURES WITH

MERMAID ACADEMY

Isla *and* Bubble
Cora *and* Sparkle
Maya *and* Rainbow
Amber *and* Flash

MERMAID ACADEMY
Cora and Sparkle

JULIE SYKES and
LINDA CHAPMAN
illustrated by **LUCY TRUMAN**

A STEPPING STONE BOOK™
Random House 🏠 New York

Sale of this book without a front cover may be unauthorized. If the book is coverless, it may have been reported to the publisher as "unsold or destroyed" and neither the author nor the publisher may have received payment for it.

This is a work of fiction. Names, characters, places, and incidents either are the product of the authors' imagination or are used fictitiously. Any resemblance to actual persons, living or dead, events, or locales is entirely coincidental.

Text copyright © 2023 by Julie Sykes and Linda Chapman
Cover art and interior illustrations copyright © 2023 by Lucy Truman

All rights reserved. Published in the United States by Random House Children's Books, a division of Penguin Random House LLC, New York. Originally published in paperback in the United Kingdom by Nosy Crow Ltd, London, in 2023.

Random House and the colophon are registered trademarks and A Stepping Stone Book and the colophon are trademarks of Penguin Random House LLC.

Visit us on the Web!
rhcbooks.com

Educators and librarians, for a variety of teaching tools, visit us at RHTeachersLibrarians.com

Library of Congress Cataloging-in-Publication Data is available upon request.
ISBN 978-0-593-89974-8 (trade)—ISBN 978-0-593-89975-5 (lib. bdg.)—
ISBN 978-0-593-89976-2 (ebook)

Printed in the United States of America
10 9 8 7 6 5 4 3 2 1
First American Edition

Random House Children's Books supports the First Amendment and celebrates the right to read.

Penguin Random House values and supports copyright. Copyright fuels creativity, encourages diverse voices, promotes free speech, and creates a vibrant culture. Thank you for buying an authorized edition of this book and for complying with copyright laws by not reproducing, scanning, or distributing any part of it in any form without permission. You are supporting writers and allowing Penguin Random House to continue to publish books for every reader. Please note that no part of this book may be used or reproduced in any manner for the purpose of training artificial intelligence technologies or systems.

For Heather Wright, who
puts the rock into reading
–J.S. and L.C.

To Elsie, with love x
–L.T.

CHAPTER 1

"Cora, over here!" Amber waved at her from near the fin-ball goal.

It was the last minute of the game. Cora saw three mermaids from Ocean Mist dorm charging down the field toward her. She quickly flicked the ball to Sparkle, her dolphin, who headed it on to Amber.

Amber caught the ball with her tail and whacked it at the goal. It flew past the outstretched fingertips of Mila, the Ocean Mist goalkeeper, and hit the back of the net.

"Yay!" Amber cried, spinning around in

delight. "Three goals to two! Moon Pearl dorm wins!"

Whooping loudly, Cora and her dorm-mates, Isla, Maya, and Amber high-fived each other. Then they high-finned their dolphins, Sparkle, Bubble, Rainbow, and Flash.

Cora felt happiness rush through her. Just a few weeks ago, she'd been nervous about starting at Mermaid Academy. She loved her home and old

school and didn't like it when things changed, but now she was really glad she'd come here. Having a dolphin to partner with was awesome, and the more she got to know Amber, Maya, and Isla, the more she liked them. The only thing that could make it more perfect would be if she and her twin sister, Isobel, were in the same dorm.

Cora glanced to where Isobel was talking with the rest of her Ocean Mist dorm-mates. Seeing the disappointment on her twin's face, Cora's happiness faded. It felt weird being on different teams. "Well played, Issy!" she called, swimming over.

"You too. It was a great game," said Isobel.

"Your two goals were amazing."

Isobel smiled. "Thanks, Cor."

"Maybe we could change the teams next time," Cora suggested hopefully. "Have two from our dorm and two from yours."

Isobel gave her a look like she had just suggested cuddling a porcupine fish. "Why would we do that? It's much more fun if we play dorm against dorm. Rematch soon?" she called as Cora's Moon Pearl dorm-mates came swimming over to join them.

"Definitely!" said Isla.

"If you think you can face losing again, of course," teased Amber.

"Flippers to that! It'll be your turn to lose next time," said Isobel, grinning.

Their good-natured teasing was interrupted by the sound of a distant conch shell being blown. It meant that afternoon classes were about to start. "We'd better get a swish on!" said Maya. "We have Mer Culture this afternoon with Ms. Seafern. We don't want to be late."

"We have Oceans of the World with Ms. Samphire," said Isobel. "See you later!"

"Bye, Issy!" called Cora, but her twin was already zooming off. Cora sighed. She wished that Issy missed her just a little bit more. Before they'd come to the academy, they'd done everything together.

"What's wrong, Cora?" Sparkle said, nudging her.

Cora smiled at the pretty light-blue dolphin. She was so happy that Sparkle had agreed to be her dolphin partner when they started at the academy. Sparkle always sensed what Cora was feeling, and she was a really good listener.

"It's just Issy," Cora said. "We've always been best friends, but now she spends most of her time with her dorm. I miss her."

"You'll see her more during the break," said Sparkle. "I love my two sisters and my brother, but I hardly see them here at school. They have their friends, and I have mine. We still have lots of

fun once we're back home with Mom, Dad, and all our aunties, uncles, and cousins!"

"Mmm," said Cora, imagining how busy and lively Sparkle's home must be. "I guess it's different because Issy and I are twins, and there are only the two of us."

Sparkle nuzzled her. "Just because Issy is spending time with the rest of her dorm doesn't mean she likes you less. She might have new friends, but she'll never have another twin sister."

"Thanks, Sparkle," Cora said, kissing her head. "You always know what to say. I'm so glad we're partners. I hope we bond soon!"

"Me too!" said Sparkle.

When a student and a dolphin bonded, their tail fins changed color to match. Isla and her dolphin, Bubble, had already bonded and both of them now had violet-and-pink tail fins.

Isla had also discovered her magic—she was able to make streams of bubbles appear whenever she wanted. Every merperson had their own special type of magic. Cora couldn't wait to find out what hers would be!

"We should catch up with the others," Sparkle said, glancing to where Maya, Isla, and Amber were swimming toward the school. "We'll have to link up. Grab my fin, Cora!"

Cora took hold of Sparkle's back fin and felt a rush of magical energy. They flicked their tails, and the next moment they were racing through the water at double speed.

Cora's thick light-blue hair streamed out behind her. She laughed in delight as they plunged into

a school of tiny blue-and-yellow fish. They raced with them for a few moments before the cloud of fish swirled away. Happiness fizzed through her as she and Sparkle zoomed through the turquoise water. Even though she couldn't be with Issy all the time, Cora loved being a student at Mermaid Academy!

CHAPTER 2

The academy was built out of rainbow-colored coral in a place of powerful magic, where the four largest oceans of the world met. Its buildings surrounded a large circular courtyard called the Singing Circle. The windows had no glass and were open to the sea, with friendly fish drifting in and out.

On the ground floor there was a large dining hall, an art studio, music rooms, and the Grand Cavern, where the students had assemblies. It was also where the head teacher, Dr. Oceania, had her office. The two floors above had classrooms and teachers' offices. The floors at the top housed the dorms for all the students.

Cora and her friends swam to a window on the first floor and dove in, almost bumping into a surprised Napoleon fish that was on its way out. The merboys from Sea Jet dorm and the mermaids from Lilac Star dorm were already settling down on driftwood benches, ready for the class to start.

"Phew! That was close!" Maya whispered to Cora, sitting down at their bench just as their teacher, Ms. Seafern, entered the room.

"Ahem!" said Ms. Seafern, looking at Amber, who was still leaning out of the window chatting with Flash. "Are you planning on joining us, Amber, or would you rather have a behavior point?"

Amber grinned, unbothered by the teacher's stern tone. "Sorry. I'll sit down," she said, swimming over and sitting between Maya and Isla.

Maya gave Cora a worried look. Amber never seemed bothered when she got in trouble, but Cora knew that the thought of getting behavior points upset Maya, who hated being in trouble. The students earned sea-star points for good work, but every behavior point meant one sea-star point was taken away from their dorm's total!

Ms. Seafern was a tall, elegant mermaid. Her purple-and-red-streaked hair was up in a bun, the loose strands pulled back with two jeweled hair clips. "Today's lesson is on mer clans," she said. "Take out your sea scrolls and squink pens and take notes, please. There will be a test in two weeks."

"Yay! I like tests," Maya whispered.

"You're as weird as a whooper fish!" Amber whispered back.

Cora grinned. She agreed with Amber. The only tests she liked were musical ones. She touched

the small silver flute that she always carried with her in her seaweed bag.

"So how many mer clans can we name?" asked Ms. Seafern.

Hands shot up all around the room.

"Silvertail."

"Arrowswift!"

"Seabright."

"Starshine."

"Wavesong!"

The students called out clan names as Ms. Seafern pointed at them. For many years the clans had lived apart, but a pioneering mermaid named Marina Star had decided that it would be much better if the clans worked together to protect the oceans, sharing their knowledge and magic. She had started Mermaid Academy so that young members of the different clans could study together. They could train to be guardians of their world while forming friendships that would hopefully last a lifetime.

"Excellent," said Ms. Seafern, nodding. "Any more? Yes, Isla?"

"The Mal Mer," Isla said.

Everyone's pens paused above their scrolls, and Ms. Seafern froze. The Mal Mer was a secretive clan and the only one that did not send students to the academy. Their home, the Malmari Ocean, bordered the Shining Sea, where Cora's clan lived. The Mal Mer were said to be mean and dangerous, so Cora and her clan stayed well away from the boundary. Her dad had crossed it once, though, to help an injured turtle. He had been shocked to find that the Malmari Ocean was a barren wasteland with dying coral and very little sea life.

"Is it true that the Mal Mer never leave their own ocean?" asked Millie from Lilac Star.

"That certainly used to be true," said Ms. Seafern. "However, there have been recent sightings of them in other oceans. If you happen to see one of the Mal Mer clan, I would advise you to swim away quickly. Some of them can control minds and will use their power to make other merfolk and sea creatures do their bidding."

"How would you know if someone was one of the Mal Mer?" asked Lyla, also from Lilac Star.

"By their tails," said Ms. Seafern. "The clan like to polish their scales with an oil they drain from the petrol fish. They often add silver decorations too. The Mal Mer love shiny and precious things. Some even decorate their tails with the very rare purple-spotted barnacle."

A gasp rippled through the class. "Is that true?" Maya asked.

Ms. Seafern nodded. "Sadly, yes. They also keep sea creatures in tanks."

"That's so cruel!" exclaimed Lyla, looking horrified. None of the other clans would ever keep a sea creature in captivity—or wear one!

A memory flashed into Cora's mind. A few weeks ago, in their first few days at the school, she and her dorm-mates had found a herd of woolly seahorses trapped in a cave. Could that have been the work of the Mal Mer?

Ms. Seafern looked around. "That's enough about the Mal Mer. Please don't worry about them. Let's focus on the clans that do work together. Who can tell me where the Swifttail clan lives?"

The lesson continued, and Cora enjoyed learning about the different clans and where they came from. At the end of the class, Ms. Seafern made an announcement. "For the rest of this term, Dr. Oceania has decided that on Fridays, rather than normal lessons, you will all take part in an

enrichment activity." She handed out sheets of sea parchment with a list of clubs. "Clubs start tomorrow. Please read through the descriptions and make your choice by then."

An excited murmur rose as the students read the list. Cora studied the piece of paper.

Coral Club with Ms. Rocksea
Use the Magical Globe to visit reefs around the world and learn how to care for rare corals.

Medicine Club with Mr. Wakame
Learn how to use magical sea plants and herbs for good and to help merfolk and sea life.

Art Club with Mr. Marimo
Painting and drawing for all abilities. Includes field trips to draw landscapes.

Wildlife Club with Mr. Nori
Learn about sea life and help to care for injured fish and animals at the wildlife sanctuary.

Music Club with Ms. Melody

Singing and playing different musical instruments to create magic mer-music. Open to all abilities.

That's the one for me! Cora thought immediately. Her mom said that Cora had a natural talent for music. When she played her flute, sea creatures always gathered around.

An exciting thought popped into Cora's head. Issy played the lyre—a small handheld harp—and they'd talked about learning new instruments at school. If she and Issy both took Music Club, they could spend every Friday together!

Isla leaned across Maya. "I'm going to join Coral Club."

"Me too. It sounds amazing!" said Amber.

Maya nodded hard. "And me. I'd love to learn more about reefs and corals."

Isla looked at Cora. "How about you, Cora?"

"I love music, so I'm going to join the Music Club," Cora said.

Her friends' faces fell.

"Oh, Cora!" Amber protested. "Don't be a solo sailfish. Come to Coral Club with us."

"It'll be much more fun if we do the same thing," said Isla. She put her hands together. "Pleeeease, Cora."

Cora hesitated. Going to different places and learning about corals did sound fun, and she hated upsetting people. Should she change her mind? But then she thought of Issy. "Sorry, but I really do want to join Music Club."

"Well, in that case, that's what you should do," said Maya firmly.

Amber opened her mouth to protest, but Maya jumped in. "Cora shouldn't choose Coral Club just because we're doing it. She should pick something she wants to do."

Isla smiled at Cora. "Agreed. We'll miss you, but we'll tell you all about it. And you can play musical instruments for us. Deal?"

"Deal!" said Cora, with a happy flick of her tail.

CHAPTER 3

"Issy!" Cora raced across the dining hall. It was dinnertime, and Isobel was carrying a tray of food over to the long table where her dorm-mates, Mila, Emmie, and Abi, had left a space for her.

"Oh, hi, Cora," Isobel said, stopping and treading water. "Dinner looks good, doesn't it? Seaweed lasagna and wild-garlic bread and foamberry mousse for dessert. Yum!"

The meal looked delicious, but Cora had more important things on her mind. "Have you heard about the enrichment activities for tomorrow? We can join the Music Club together. How swishy will that be?" She beamed at her twin.

Isobel looked awkward. "Oh, sorry, Cora. I'm already doing Medicine Club."

Cora felt as if her tail had just been plonked in a bucket of Arctic ice. "Medicine Club?" she echoed, hardly able to believe it. "But why? You love music!"

Isobel shrugged. "I wanted to try something new, and it'll be cool to learn about the magic healing powers of sea plants. Mila, Emmie, and Abi think so too. We really wanted to do a club together, so that's what we chose. Your dorm is doing Music Club with you, aren't they?"

Cora felt close to tears. "They're doing Coral Club," she whispered.

Isobel looked uncomfortable. "Why don't you change your mind and go to Coral Club with them?"

"Or I could do Medicine Club with you," said Cora quickly.

Isobel looked surprised. "Well, yes, if you want. But are you sure? It doesn't seem like your kind of thing. You've never been that interested in plants." Issy had often helped their mom in their garden, but Cora had preferred to play her flute or read.

"I like plants," said Cora, twisting her hands together nervously. "And at least we'd be together. I hardly ever see you now."

Issy bit her lip. "Things are different here at school."

"Bella! Hurry up and sit down!" Mila called.

Bella? Cora blinked. Isobel had never been called Bella, she'd always been either Isobel or Issy.

"Coming!" Issy called. She smiled at Cora. "I guess I'll see you at Medicine Club, then?"

Cora nodded and slowly swam over to join the line for food. Amber and Maya had almost reached the serving counter.

"Cora!" shouted Amber, waving her over. "We've saved you a space."

Cora went to join them, but an older student with long black hair and a badge pinned to her sparkly top swam in front of her. She held her hand up. "No cutting the line."

"She's not. She's in our dorm. Let her join us, Marianna," Amber pleaded.

Marianna shook her head. "Go to the back of the line," she ordered Cora. "And the next time you try to cut, I'll give you a behavior point."

Cora blushed as she swam to the end of the line. Her appetite was gone, and all she wanted now was to go see Sparkle. Rather than filling a tray with food, she took a sea vegetable spring roll and swam over to the table where Maya, Isla, and Amber were sitting.

"Where's your food?" said Isla.

"I'm not very hungry. I'm going to see if I can find Sparkle," said Cora.

Isla looked concerned. "Are you okay?"

"Yes, thanks," Cora fibbed.

"Do you want us to come with you?" asked Maya.

"No, I'll be fine." Cora avoided everyone's eyes. "I just want some time with Sparkle."

They nodded. They all liked having one-on-one time with their dolphins.

Cora swam away, eager to escape from the hustle and bustle of the dining hall.

Sparkle was playing tag with the other dolphins in the Singing Circle, but as soon as she spotted Cora, she left the game. "Hi, Cora. Where are the others?"

"Still eating, but I wasn't hungry," Cora said.

Sparkle frowned. "What's the matter?"

"Nothing," Cora muttered.

Sparkle studied her for a moment. "Do you want to go for a swim?"

Cora nodded, and they swam into the school grounds through the pink coral arch. It was being chomped on by the black-silver-and-red nibbler fish that were always snacking on some part of the academy's coral walls. Mermaids were supposed to shoo them away, but Cora was too upset to bother.

Sparkle shot worried glances at her, but Cora didn't speak until they reached Tranquility Garden. It was a peaceful area where shell paths

twisted around statues of famous mermen and mermaids and beds of white-and-pink anemones, their feathery fronds waving in the currents. They reached a quiet area beside the statue of a wise-looking merman stroking a manatee and stopped.

"What's wrong, Cora?" said Sparkle. "You look really upset."

"It's Issy. She won't do Music Club with me." Cora explained about the clubs, finishing with a sigh. "She loves music, so why has she decided to do Medicine Club? It sounds boring."

"Maybe she wants to try something new now that she's here at school," said Sparkle. "It can be fun to try different things, and it's normal for people to change as they get older."

Cora frowned. She didn't want Issy to change. Sparkle nuzzled her. "What will you do? Will you go to Music Club on your own or do Coral Club with the others?"

"Neither," said Cora. "I'm going to go to Medicine Club with Issy."

Sparkle looked surprised. "But shouldn't you choose a club you want to do?"

Cora shrugged. "I don't care about the club. I just want to be with Issy."

Sparkle hesitated as if there was something she wanted to say, but then she seemed to change her mind. "Well, if that's what you want and it will make you happy to do Medicine Club, I'm glad you've chosen it. I don't like you being sad."

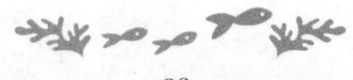

Cora leaned her head against Sparkle's and felt her unhappiness fade away. "Thanks, Sparkle. I'm so lucky you're my dolphin."

Sparkle kissed her on the nose. "And I'm so lucky you're my mermaid! Now, the others said they wanted to go to the playground after dinner. How about we see if we can find them?"

"Okay," said Cora.

They swam through the school grounds, reaching the playground at the same time as Isla, Amber, Maya, and their dolphins. Cora soon forgot about Issy and the clubs as she bounced on the giant sponge trampolines, rode the twisting mother-of-pearl slides, and was flung around on the spinning clams with her friends.

"This is fun, isn't it?" said Sparkle, her eyes shining.

"Oh yes!" Cora exclaimed.

CHAPTER 4

The next day, Cora saw Issy setting off for the Medicine Club with her dorm-mates and hurried to catch them. They were all laughing about a prank that Ocean Mist had played on Lilac Star the night before.

Issy grinned. "It was so funny! I actually thought Harper was going to faint."

Abi said in a creepy voice, "Beware the poisoned puffffffer!"

Issy, Mila, and Emmie burst out laughing.

"Why is that so funny?" Cora asked Issy.

Issy grinned. "I guess you had to be there." She

turned to the others. "We should play another prank soon." They started talking eagerly about what they could do, and Cora dropped behind.

She wondered what Isla, Maya, and Amber were doing and where the Magical Globe had taken them. It showed every ocean, sea, lake, and lagoon and could be used to travel anywhere in the underwater world. Her dorm-mates had been very excited as they got ready, putting on their adventure jackets and making sure they had bags with them so they could bring back coral cuttings if needed.

"We'll miss you!" they'd said, hugging Cora as they left.

Swimming along on her own, Cora found herself missing them too. *It'll be fine once Medicine Club starts,* she told herself. *Issy and I will be partners, and we'll work together all day.*

But when Mr. Wakame told them to choose

partners, Mila quickly grabbed Isobel's hand. "Bella! You said that you'd go with me."

Isobel glanced between Mila and Cora. "Um..."

"We'll need one group to be a three," Mr. Wakame said.

Isobel looked relieved. "Let's all go together."

Cora's heart sank—and the day didn't improve after that. She didn't find the club that interesting, and her mind kept drifting as Mr. Wakame talked about the properties of the different plants. By the time they actually started to make seaweed bandages out of kelp, algae, and heal-fast, Cora didn't know how much heal-fast to add. In the end, Issy suggested it might be best if she and Mila finished the bandages without her.

Cora watched them from a nearby rock. This was the opposite of what she'd planned! Frustrated, she slapped her tail down and a mini whirlwave shot away from her. The tiny cone-shaped swirl of water spun toward Mila and Isobel. It knocked over the tripod and sent the clamshell on top of it flying.

"Cora!" Isobel exclaimed as Mila cried out at the sight of their mixture floating away on the ocean current.

"Sorry!" gasped Cora. "I don't know what happened."

"Now we have to start all over again!" Mila groaned.

Cora felt awful. Medicine Club wasn't working out as she had hoped.

Lunchtime was better. Everyone sat together and the talk turned to magic.

"I can't wait to find out what powers I have," said Isobel.

"Will you and Cora find your magic at the exact same time because you're twins?" said Emmie curiously.

"I doubt it," said Isobel. "I always do things first."

"Actually, I played a tune on the flute first," Cora pointed out.

"You did." Isobel chuckled. "Can you remember how mad I was?"

Cora could. Isobel hadn't spoken to her for two whole days. Afterward, Isobel had refused to play

her own flute and had chosen to learn the lyre instead.

"Who's older?" asked Abi. "Is it you, Bella?"

"Yep," said Issy.

"Only by two minutes," Cora was quick to remind her.

The twins grinned at each other and for a moment Cora felt a warm glow, but that feeling soon faded as Issy and the others started talking about a pillow fight they'd had the night before. She couldn't join in, so she fell into silence, wrapping her arms around her tail and feeling like an outsider once again.

"Hi, Cora! Did you have fun at Medicine Club?" asked Sparkle, zooming over to meet her when the clubs had ended.

"It was okay," said Cora. She'd come back with some of the healing bandages. Issy and Mila had insisted that she take them even though she hadn't helped much.

Isla, Amber, and Maya came swimming out of the Grand Cavern looking sea-swept but happy.

"How was your day?" Cora called as their dolphins greeted them.

"Incredible!" said Maya, her eyes shining. "The Magical Globe took us to a coral reef in the Glass Ocean where some very rare and special corals grow."

"Some of the coral had been badly damaged," said Isla. "Huge chunks of it had disappeared. Ms. Rocksea said that a large group of thorny starfish must have been feeding on it."

"Only a gigantic group could have done so much damage," said Maya thoughtfully. "We took some cuttings, and Ms. Rocksea has taken them to her coral nursery. She has growing magic. She's going to use it on the cuttings, and when they are big enough, we'll use them to repair the reef. She said it shouldn't take long."

"There were so many creatures on the reef!" said Amber. She nudged Isla. "Do you remember that massive wrasse fish we saw?"

"The one hiding at the back of that cave?" said Isla. "I almost jumped out of my skin when it moved!"

"And what about that group of purple-ringed jellyfish?" said Maya. "I thought we were going to get stung!"

"We had to zoom out of the way so fast!" said Isla.

As the three of them discussed their exciting day, Cora's spirits sank. She knew they didn't mean for her to feel left out, but because she hadn't been there, she couldn't join in.

She felt a tap on her arm. It was Sparkle. "Do you want to go for a swim together?"

Cora nodded. As the others headed toward Ms. Rocksea's coral nursery, she and Sparkle slipped away.

Sparkle nuzzled Cora's arm. "You don't seem very happy. Didn't you have fun today at your club?"

Cora sighed. "Not really." She told her all about it. "I was so excited to be with Issy, but she doesn't even call herself that now. She's Bella! It's like she's a different mermaid here at school. Oh, Sparkle, I just want the old Issy back!" Cora felt a wave of unhappiness in her tummy, and she slapped her tail against a boulder. A mini whirlwave shot away from her, spinning wildly into a cluster of candy-cane coral and dissolving in a cloud of bubbles.

"Flippers!" Sparkle's eyes widened. "Where did that come from?"

"I don't know." Cora was mystified. "Something similar happened earlier when I was at Medicine Club."

Sparkle stared at her. "It could be your magic, Cora. Try that again."

Cora flicked her tail, and another whirlwave spun away from her, bigger and stronger this time. It hit a group of tube sponges, and they fell over like dominoes.

"Cora!" Sparkle exclaimed. "You have whirlwave magic!"

"Oh wow!" Cora could hardly believe it. Her older cousin, Violet, had whirlwave magic. Not only could she make whirlwaves in all sizes, she could move them exactly where she wanted them to go.

Some of the scales at the top of Cora's turquoise tail had turned silver, forming a picture of a mini whirlwave. An excited thrill ran through her, but then her delight burst like a bubble.

"I can't have found my magic!" she said, her green eyes wide. "Oh, Sparkle! Issy's going to be really upset. She was so sure that she'd get hers first."

"She won't mind that much, will she?" Sparkle said.

Cora gulped. "She will." She started rubbing at the silver scales.

"You can't rub it off," said Sparkle, nudging her hand away. "It's part of you now, Cora."

"Then I have to hide it!" Cora felt like crying. She dug in her seaweed pouch for one of Mr. Wakame's bandages and stuck it over the silver scales. "There," she said in relief. "Now I can keep my magic secret. You won't tell anyone, will you, Sparkle?"

"N-no," said Sparkle.

"What's the matter?" said Cora, seeing she looked unhappy.

"I don't think you should lie to Issy or your friends," replied Sparkle.

"I'll tell them the truth after Issy has found her magic," said Cora. She put a hand on Sparkle. "Promise you won't say anything for now?"

Sparkle hesitated.

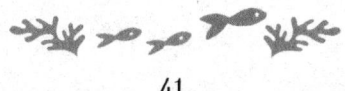

"Please, Sparkle," she begged.

Reluctantly, Sparkle nodded.

Cora kissed her, but for once Sparkle didn't kiss her back. They bobbed in the water, an uncomfortable silence stretching between them.

Cora cleared her throat. "Let's go find the others."

They swam back to the Singing Circle, neither of them saying a word.

CHAPTER 5

That evening, Amber had arranged a fin-ball rematch with Isobel's dorm. It should have been fun, but Cora was so worried that her bandage might fall off, she kept missing the ball. As Cora flicked the ball to Amber, a whirlwave shot out. Luckily, Sparkle saw it, and thinking quickly, she dove on top of it, squashing it before anyone noticed.

"Thank you!" Cora whispered.

Sparkle gave her a pleading look, but Cora shook her head. She knew Sparkle wanted her to tell the truth, but she couldn't risk making the gap between her and Issy even wider. She saw the unhappiness in Sparkle's eyes but turned away.

Later in the dorm, when everyone was getting ready for bed, Cora didn't join in the chatter.

She just jumped into her clamshell bed and burrowed under her pink blanket dotted with tiny silver moons. But it was ages before she finally fell asleep.

When Cora woke up the next morning, for a few blissful seconds she felt happy to be waking up at Mermaid Academy. Excitement flickered through her at the thought of what the day might hold, but then she remembered her magic and her heart fell. How was she going to hide it from her friends? *I'm going to have to learn to control it better,* she thought.

"It's the weekend!" Isla's voice sang out.

"No classes, just lots of fun!" said Amber, stretching.

"What are we going to do today?" said Maya.

"Play fin-ball!" said Amber. "But breakfast first." She threw back her blanket.

Cora sat up, her tummy filled with dread at the thought of the day ahead.

"Are you okay?" Maya asked her. "You don't look great."

"I have a headache," Cora lied. "I think I might stay here."

"You poor thing," said Isla in concern. "Should we get Ms. Comfrey?" Ms. Comfrey was the school nurse.

"It's okay," said Cora quickly. "I'm sure it will go away if I just rest."

They fussed around her until Cora insisted that they go down for breakfast. Alone at last, she flopped back against her pillows, wondering if she could stay in bed for the whole day!

Her friends returned, talking excitedly.

"Guess what we're doing today!" Amber exclaimed.

"Amber, shh! Cora has a headache, remember?" said Maya.

"Sorry!" said Amber, lowering her voice.

"It's okay," said Cora, feeling guilty for lying to them. "What are you up to?"

"We're going to the Glass Ocean with our dolphins," said Amber.

"Ms. Rocksea's growing magic worked," said Isla. "The coral cuttings are big enough to be replanted back to the reef, and Ms. Rocksea wants to repair the damage as soon as possible."

"How are you feeling?" Maya asked. "I'm sure you and Sparkle could ask to come, too, if you're up to it?"

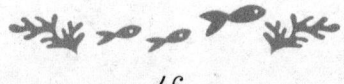

Cora longed to say yes. She really wanted to see the Glass Ocean for herself, and she knew Sparkle would love to go with her. But she couldn't take the risk of revealing her magic. "I think I'd rather stay here."

"Will you be all right on your own?" asked Isla in concern.

Cora forced a smile. "Yes. I'll be fine."

When the others left, Cora picked up her flute. Playing it usually cheered her up but not today. In the end, she gave up trying and swam to the window, looking down at the Singing Circle. Some of the younger students were playing hide-and-seek with their dolphins. A few of the older ones were taking turns playing the golden harp that stood on a pedestal in the center of the circle. Cora's heart twisted as she caught sight of Sparkle swimming slowly in circles on her own. She could tell by the way her dolphin hung her head and the way her flippers drooped that she was upset.

Cora knew it was her fault that Sparkle was sad. Though it was too late to go with the others to the Glass Ocean, she was sure there was something nice they could do together. She changed out of her pajama top. As she brushed her hair, Sparkle's head appeared at the open window.

The dolphin's eyes sparkled when she saw her. "Cora! The others said you weren't feeling well. Are you better now?"

"Yes," said Cora. "Do you want to go somewhere quiet where I can practice my magic?"

Sparkle immediately perked up. "Oh yes!"

They set off through the school grounds and

found an empty glade of giant sea fans in Tranquility Garden.

"Here goes nothing!" said Cora, excited to master her magic. She pictured a whirlwave and felt a tingle shoot across the scales of her tail. As the magic built up inside her, the tingle grew sharper. Cora flicked her tail fin hard, and a huge whirlwave erupted. It twirled across the glade like a spinning funnel, sweeping up a couple of surprised hermit crabs and whirling them around.

"Oh flippers!" Cora exclaimed as the funnel hit a sea fan and exploded into a fountain of bubbles, sending the crabs flying through the water. The crabs landed on the sandy floor, shook their claws in astonishment, and then scuttled away, peering nervously out from behind a nearby rock. "Sorry!" Cora called to them. She made a face at Sparkle. "I really do need more practice!"

She set to work, trying again and again, until at last she could control the size and speed of the whirlwaves.

"Swishy!" said Sparkle. She clapped her flippers as Cora sent a mini whirlwave dancing in and out of the sea fans. Then Cora made it rise upward until, with a flick of her tail, it dissolved. "That was amazing!"

Cora flopped down. "I'm worn out. Doing magic is hard work, but I think I'll be able to stop whirlwaves from randomly appearing so I can keep my magic secret."

Sparkle sighed. "It would be much easier to just tell everyone."

"I will—as soon as Issy finds her magic," said Cora.

Sparkle frowned. "But what about your friends? Won't they be upset to know that you've kept such a big secret from them?"

"They won't find out," said Cora. "As soon as Issy gets her magic, I'll pretend that I just found mine."

"So, in other words, you'll tell another lie?" said Sparkle.

Cora swallowed. Put like that it did sound bad. "I can't upset Issy, Sparkle. Please try to understand."

For a moment, Sparkle looked as if she was going to argue, but then she sighed. "Okay. I said I'd keep your secret, so I will. Let's go back to school."

Cora's tummy felt like it was tying itself in kelp knots as they swam back. *I am doing the right thing*, she thought. *I'm doing this for Issy.*

But if it was the right thing, why did it feel so wrong?

CHAPTER 6

Isla, Amber, and Maya arrived back at lunchtime with their dolphins, and they were happy to see that Cora was feeling better. As they ate seaweed wraps, they told her all about the reef.

"We repaired the damaged areas, but more coral has been broken overnight," said Isla.

Amber nodded. "Massive chunks are gone. Ms. Rocksea decided that it definitely isn't the work of the thorny starfish."

"It looks like someone used a big knife to cut the coral away, but no mermaid or merman would do something like that," said Maya.

"It's a real mystery. I wish we could solve it," added Isla.

"You know who can help with mysteries?" said Cora.

"Who?" the others said.

"The Sea Sphinx of course!" said Cora. The Sea Sphinx was a living statue. She was half mermaid and half octopus, and she could answer any question—but only if she chose to. Even if she did answer, her answers weren't easy to understand because she only talked in riddles. But she had helped them once before when all the woolly seahorses on the school grounds had gone missing.

"That's a brilliant idea, Cora!" said Maya.

"Awesome!" agreed Isla.

"We could go see her this afternoon," suggested Cora.

Amber grinned. "Why wait? Let's get the dolphins and go right now!"

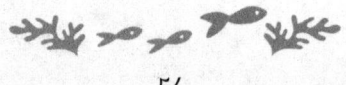

☆

The Sea Sphinx stood in the center of a small maze surrounded by white anemones. As they swam there, Cora realized how good it felt to be doing something with her dorm and their dolphins. She'd missed them that morning.

They lined up in front of the midnight-blue statue. The Sea Sphinx's marble face was cold and her head bowed. On top of her long copper-colored hair, which hung in locks down her back, she wore a shell-studded tiara.

"Greetings, oh great Sea Sphinx," said Maya politely. "We have an important question to ask if you would be so kind as to answer."

Cora gave her an admiring glance. Maya just seemed to know exactly what to say and how to say it when addressing the Sea Sphinx.

"We have been to the Glass Ocean reef," Maya continued. "We found that large chunks of the reef are being taken from it. Would you be able to tell us what is causing the damage and how we can stop it?"

There was a grinding sound as the Sea Sphinx lifted her head and fixed Maya with a glittering stare. She spoke in a harsh, gravelly voice that reminded Cora of pebbles brushing together as the waves raked over them.

"What you come to report makes me sad and cross.
Stealing rare coral is to everyone's loss.
At night there is danger when servants appear.
Their sharp swords are weapons you are wise to fear.
One becomes many; you'll need magic to fight back.
Beware of bright scales and the kindness they lack."

The Sea Sphinx closed her mouth with a loud clunk. For a moment her words seemed to echo around the center of the maze. Then the light in her eyes went out and silence fell.

"What did she mean?" said Isla.

"I don't like the sound of servants with swords," said Maya.

"Who appear at night," Amber chimed in.

"Who has servants, though?" said Cora, mystified.

Isla frowned. "I'm not sure, but it sounded like we should go to the reef at night to see what's going on. Why don't we sneak into the Grand Cavern and use the globe after dinner?"

"No, Isla!" Maya said. "It could be really dangerous. We should tell a teacher."

"We could at least go and look. Then come back and let someone know," said Isla.

"But we'd be breaking the school rules if we use the globe without permission," protested Maya.

"So?" said Amber. "I vote we break the rules."

Isla nodded. "How about you and Sparkle, Cora? Will you come with us?"

"Yes," Cora said, excited. Knowing how sad Sparkle had been earlier when they'd stayed behind, she was sure her dolphin would leap at

the chance of going on a secret trip to the Glass Ocean.

"Great! So that's three of us plus our dolphins. Maya, are you seriously going to stay behind?" Isla asked her.

Maya gave in. "No, I'll come. If it's going to be dangerous, then the more of us the better. And," she said with a note of hope in her voice, "if it's not the right thing to do, then the globe won't take us there anyway."

"But if it does," Isla said with a grin, "we're going to have an awesome nighttime adventure!"

CHAPTER 7

After dinner, Cora and her friends swam to where a thick curtain of seaweed hung over the entrance to the Grand Cavern. On the way there, Cora saw Issy with her friends. They were perched on rocks and slapping their tails hard against them.

"What are you all doing?" Cora said, pausing.

"Seb found his magic earlier today—growing magic," Issy said. "He was tapping his tail against a rock, and suddenly a sea lettuce grew. We want to see if smacking our tails works for us! Why don't you try too, Cor?"

Cora shook her head. "Um—it's okay."

"Cora! Come on!" Amber shouted.

"See you later," said Cora, diving after her dorm.

They hovered near the entrance to the Grand Cavern, waiting for a chance to slip through the curtain.

"Now," Isla whispered. "While no one's watching." She took hold of the curtain.

Suddenly there was a loud scream.

Issy! Cora swung around and saw her sister swimming in circles, wildly shaking her tail as a large crab hung on tight to her tail fin. Issy must have disturbed it by hitting its hiding place in the rock with her tail! Issy shrieked even louder as she flapped her tail, trying to dislodge the crab's painful pincers. Her friends swam around her in alarm.

"I have to help!" Cora exclaimed.

"But, Cora, this is our perfect time to go," said

Isla. "Everyone's distracted. Issy's friends will help her."

But Cora couldn't leave while her twin was hurt. "Go," she said quickly. "It's better if I hang back. Then if you haven't returned by lights-out, I can raise the alarm. Be careful!"

Before they could argue, Cora dove toward her sister.

Fast as a wave, Cora raced to Issy's side. "Stay still!" she told her sister. "You're making the crab hold on even tighter." As Issy stopped waving her tail around, Cora pulled out her flute. She started to play a lullaby their mom would sing to send them to sleep.

As the soothing notes floated through the water, the crab finally relaxed its claws. It fell from Issy's tail and scuttled over to Cora, its antennae waving in time to the music. Cora kept playing, backing slowly toward the boulder. The crab followed and, seeing its hole in the rock, crawled back inside. Cora finished the tune and lowered the flute.

"Thank you, Cor!" Issy called gratefully, massaging her sore tail.

Cora hugged her sister. At the same time, Marianna and her prefect friend, Tinto, swam over. Tinto raised an eyebrow at Issy as he shot her an amused grin.

"What a racket!" Marianna sniffed. "Was that really necessary?"

"Yes," said Mila, putting her arm around Issy's shoulders. "The pinch of a crab's claw really hurts!"

"Let's go back to the dorm," said Abi. "I have some new shell clips. We could do each other's hair."

"And I have some hair gems we can use for decoration," said Emmie.

She linked arms with Issy, and they started to swim away.

Cora was about to follow them when Sparkle nudged her. "There's still time for us to catch up with the others, Cora."

"I can't leave Issy," protested Cora.

"You heard what her friends said. They're going to their dorm."

"But she'll want me with her as well," argued Cora. "Issy, wait!" she called. "I'll come too."

Issy glanced back. "Don't worry, Cor. My tail is only a little bit bruised, but thanks again. It was quick thinking to use your flute to make the crab let go." She gave Cora a grateful smile and allowed the others to pull her away.

Cora stared after Issy until Sparkle swam up in front of her. "Cora, can we talk?"

"Sure," said Cora in surprise. "About what?"

Sparkle led the way to the quiet spot near the entrance to the Grand Cavern. Once they were on their own, she said, "Cora, I know you and Issy are close, but I think you should concentrate on new friends while you're at school. Issy seems really happy." Cora opened her mouth to protest, but Sparkle rushed on. "By following her around, you're missing out on all the fun you could be having with Isla, Amber, Maya—and with me." She nuzzled Cora. "I'm sorry. I can't stay quiet about this anymore. I hate seeing you make yourself so unhappy."

Part of Cora wanted to argue, to tell Sparkle that she was wrong, but deep down she knew it was true. Issy was clearly having a great time with her new friends. If Cora kept trying to hang around on the outskirts of Issy's group instead of taking the time to get to know her own dormmates, she was just going to make herself more and more miserable.

"Cora?" said Sparkle anxiously. She swam closer so they were face to face. Then she stared deep into Cora's eyes. "Do you mind me telling you what I'm thinking?"

"No," said Cora, touching Sparkle's cheek. "I want us to always tell each other what we're thinking and feeling. And"—she swallowed as she admitted the truth—"you're right. I've been hanging around Issy way too much. I'm glad I stayed and helped her tonight when I thought she was in trouble. But from now on, unless she *really* needs me, I'm going to concentrate on making my own friends, in my dorm."

Sparkle looked relieved. "I know they'll be really pleased if you start to spend more time with them. They all like you a lot!"

"I wish we were with them now," said Cora, imagining her friends on their adventure on a distant reef.

Sparkle glanced at the seaweed curtain that covered the entrance to the Grand Cavern. "It's not too late to follow them."

Hope flared in Cora. Could they still go?

Sparkle swam to the curtain and, after a quick check to make sure no one was watching, nudged it aside with her nose. "Well?" she said eagerly. "Shall we try?"

Cora dove through the gap. "Glass Ocean, here we come!" she exclaimed.

CHAPTER 8

The Grand Cavern was lit by lanterns of green mermaid fire. The Magical Globe was suspended above Dr. Oceania's chair in the center of the room. It showed all the bodies of water in the merfolk's world—oceans, seas, lagoons, fjords—the names of each standing out in dark-blue writing. A shiver ran down Cora's spine as she noticed a black cloud hiding one particular ocean—the Malmari, where the Mal Mer lived. "I hope we never have reason to go there," she whispered to Sparkle as they swam around the globe, reading the other labels.

"Here!" Cora said, pointing at the Glass Ocean. "I think I need to touch you with one hand and the ocean with the other while I ask the Magical Globe to take us there. If it agrees, then the magic will work."

"Let's do it!" said Sparkle eagerly.

Touching one hand to Sparkle's back, Cora put her other hand on the Glass Ocean. Its label suddenly glowed gold, and she felt magic tingling in her fingertips.

"Please take us to the Glass Ocean, to the place where our friends are trying to solve the mystery of the missing coral," she said, choosing her words carefully. She didn't want the magic to drop her miles away from the others!

The tingling grew stronger and stronger until Cora felt like she was glowing. "Sparkle! I think it's working. Get ready to—" She broke off as darkness engulfed her and she began to tumble over and over. It was exactly as Cora had always imagined dropping down a hole in the ocean floor would feel. She screamed, but even as the sound left her mouth, she felt herself turn the right way up and a tiny version of the Magical Globe appeared in her hand. Cora looked around and saw that she and Sparkle had arrived on a huge coral reef. The crystal-clear waters were dimly lit by the moon shining high above.

Cora slipped the globe into her bag, knowing

she would need it to return to the school. Then she slowly spun around. "Oh wow!" she breathed. The reef stretched in all directions, covered by living corals of different shapes, sizes, and colors growing on top of ancient gray coral. There were thickets of branching staghorn coral, fields of round bubble coral, branches of prickly fir-tree coral, and so many other corals that Cora had never seen before. *It's very quiet,* Cora thought, feeling puzzled. Coral reefs should be filled with life. While they were quieter at night, there were usually some creatures to be seen.

"It's so empty," she whispered to Sparkle, a prickle of unease running through her scales.

Sparkle nodded. "It's not like the reefs I know. I wonder where the others are."

Cora caught sight of a movement in the distance. It looked like a shadowy tail fin slipping

behind a cluster of giant sea fans. Was it one of her friends?

"Hey!" she called, swimming toward the sea fans. "Isla? Amber? Maya?" An ice-cold wave swept over the scales of her tail. It was an odd feeling and very uncomfortable. A memory stirred in Cora's mind. She'd felt something similar once before, but she couldn't remember when.

She reached the sea fans, but no one was there. It must have been a trick of the light. Turning back toward Sparkle, she saw something small and shiny lying at the base of the sea fans. She picked it up. It was shaped like a scale, but it was made of thin silver metal. She turned it over in her hands.

"Cora, why don't you play your flute and see if any creatures come out?" called Sparkle. "Then I can ask them if they've seen any mermaids."

"Good idea," said Cora. Dolphins couldn't talk with other sea creatures, but they could communicate with each other a little using whistles and squeaks. She slipped the shiny silver object into her bag to look at later and took out her flute. Lifting it to her lips, she played a lilting tune. At first, nothing happened. Then, after a minute, a couple of orange-and-white clown fish swam out from behind a large anemone, a blue eel poked its head out of a hole in the coral, and a small turtle peeped out of a nearby cave.

"I'll see if they can understand me," said Sparkle. She spoke in a series of whistles, clicks, and squeaks and motioned at Cora.

The creatures shot back into their hiding places.

"What did you say?" said Cora in surprise.

"I asked if they'd seen any other mermaids, and they just disappeared," said Sparkle.

Cora played her flute again. After a few bars, the turtle slowly peeped out. Cora played quietly as Sparkle spoke to it in whistles again.

The turtle paused and glided out of its hiding place, waving a flipper at them to come closer. It spoke in clicks and a few hoarse barks. "The turtle says it has seen our friends and we should follow it," said Sparkle.

The turtle led the way through the silent, empty reef, gliding around the coral formations. After a little while, it stopped and pointed with its flipper toward a group of coral caves. The turtle clicked its tongue at Sparkle.

"It's saying they went that way," said Sparkle.

The turtle made a chirping noise at Sparkle and then, with a wave of its flipper, turned around and swam quickly away.

"What did it say as it left?" asked Cora.

Sparkle gave her a worried look. "It sounded like 'Get your friends out of here before it's too late.'"

Cora felt a stab of alarm as she remembered what the Sea Sphinx had said about servants with swords. The coral world was very beautiful, but she was beginning to feel more and more worried about being there. "We'd better find the others as fast as we can!"

CHAPTER 9

Cora pointed into the distance. She could just see a tail fin poking out of a cave. "Over there, is that one of our friends?"

"Yes! Come on!" said Sparkle.

"Actually, Sparkle, wait!" said Cora suddenly. There was something about the shadowy tail that didn't look right. It was swinging from side to side, propelling the creature it belonged to into the cave. Suddenly Cora had a horrible thought. A mermaid's tail fin didn't move from side to side like that, but up and down, the same way as a dolphin's. Her voice dropped to a worried whisper. "Sparkle, that's a shark!"

Most sharks weren't a threat to mermaids or dolphins, but there were a few, like sword sharks and wolf sharks, that would eat anything when they were hungry. "Do you think it's a nice shark or a scary one?" she whispered.

Sparkle's eyes widened. "I don't know."

Cora looked around and saw a huge purple sponge shaped like a giant vase. "Quick! Let's hide just in case!" They dove inside the sponge.

The shark swam back out of the cave, its smooth, muscular body moving from side to side as it cut through the water. Peeping over the edge of the vase sponge, Cora shared a worried look with Sparkle. She recognized that long sword-shaped nose. The shark was a scary, predatory one!

"Keep very still," she mouthed to Sparkle.

The sword shark swam toward a branching

colony of magenta fir-tree coral. Another creature, with a long, thin gray body and huge jaws, slithered after it. *A gulper eel,* thought Cora, feeling confused. She was taught that gulper eels only lived in the deep sea. What was this one doing here?

The sword shark swam up to the coral and swung its head to one side. Cora stopped herself from squeaking in shock as it suddenly smashed its long swordlike snout into the base of the beautiful rare coral.

CRACK! Big pieces broke off. The gulper eel opened its huge mouth and caught them.

SMACK! CRACK!

Cora could hardly believe what she was seeing as the shark slashed at the coral, only stopping when the gulper eel's jaws were full. The eel turned and whipped away through the water.

Cora's thoughts raced. She'd never heard of a

shark destroying a reef. It must have been what the Sea Sphinx had meant when she'd talked about servants with sharp swords. But why *servants?* Sharks were no one's servants. And where was the eel taking the coral? *I have to find the others quickly,* she thought. *They need to know about this.*

The shark left the coral and swam toward

the vase sponge. Hardly daring to breathe, Cora and Sparkle stayed very still. The shark had almost passed them by when it stopped, lifting its snout as if scenting the water. It opened its mouth slightly, revealing razor-sharp teeth. Cora felt her blood turn icy. Sharks had an extremely good sense of smell.

Please swim on! she thought desperately.

Just then a second gulper eel came swimming around a cluster of staghorn coral.

Seeing the shark, the eel motioned with its head to follow, then turned around. The shark lowered its head and hurried after the eel. Together, they silently disappeared out of sight.

Cora's breath left her in a rush. "Trembling tuna, I thought that shark had smelled us!"

"Me too," said Sparkle shakily. "It was really scary. Did you see its teeth?"

"They were huge!" said Cora. "Let's find the others and tell them to get out of here."

They swam out of the sponge and set off to the caves. Cora didn't want to risk calling her friends' names in case the shark heard and came back. She and Sparkle peered into the first couple of caves. The sides and roof were encrusted with beautiful sponges and rare corals, but there was no sign of Isla, Amber, Maya, or their dolphins. However, as they swam toward the opening that led into the fourth and largest cave, Cora heard something that made her heart leap—it was Amber's voice floating out!

"Please, Maya, we can't go back yet. We haven't solved the mystery!"

Cora dove through the narrow entrance and swam down a short tunnel that ended in a beautiful cavern. Coral columns reached from the floor to the ceiling, and golden sun corals and colorful sponges covered the walls. Isla, Maya, Amber, and their three dolphins were peering at an area where large chunks of coral had been cut away.

"There you are!"

Hearing Cora's voice, they all swung around, their faces lighting up.

"Cora!" exclaimed Isla.

"Oh wow, you came after all!" said Amber.

Maya grinned. "Isn't this place awesome?

Though really different at night. It's so quiet. Do you like it?"

Cora ignored their questions. "We have to go!" she exclaimed as the dolphins crowded around Sparkle, greeting her with happy whistles. "There's a sword shark close by!" The expressions on her friends' faces changed to looks of alarm. "It's the creature with a sword that the Sea Sphinx talked about," she went on. "I saw it damaging the coral."

"A sword shark's been destroying the reef?" said Isla, shocked. "But why?"

"I don't know, but please can we just go and talk about it back at school?" begged Cora. She took the mini globe out of her bag. "Did you also get a globe when you arrived?"

"Yes," said Amber, taking a matching one from her bag. "It appeared in my hand. We all need to be touching it, and touching our dolphins too."

"Two mermaids and their dolphins to each globe," said Maya.

Cora held out her globe to Isla since she was nearest to her, but she realized that Isla seemed to have frozen. Cora followed her gaze into the tunnel and took a sharp breath.

Coming toward them down the tunnel was the sword shark—and it looked hungry!

CHAPTER 10

We're going to be eaten! thought Cora, fear gripping her as she stared at the shark.

Isla pushed in front of her. "Back off, Pointy Teeth!" she shouted bravely. "Or I'll use my magic, and you really won't like that."

But the shark didn't stop.

"Okay, then. Take that!" Isla smacked her tail on the floor of the tunnel. A jet of bubbles shot away from her and hit the shark, throwing it backward. Its beady eyes were round with shock as it twisted and turned, fighting the current of bubbles.

"Get the globes ready to use, and then I'll join you," cried Isla, keeping the jet of bubbles trained on the shark.

The other mermaids and dolphins didn't need to be told twice. Maya, Rainbow, and Flash crowded around Amber while Bubble hovered uncertainly between Isla, Cora, and Sparkle.

Isla continued to blast a stream of bubbles at the shark. Then suddenly she gasped. "Clattering clams!"

She shot backward and bumped into Cora and Amber, causing them both to drop the globes. A wave of terror swept over Cora as she looked around and saw what had caused Isla to retreat so quickly. Five more sword sharks had appeared in the tunnel entrance!

Shock made Isla's magic splutter, then fail. The few remaining bubbles popped and disappeared as the sharks started swimming down the tunnel.

"Get back, everyone!" she yelled.

"One becomes many," squeaked Maya as the mermaids and their dolphins sped to the back of the cave. "It's what the Sea Sphinx said, and it must be why the reef is so quiet. All the other creatures have been hiding from the sharks."

"But sword sharks don't usually hunt together," said Amber. "What's going on?"

"Whatever it is, I don't like it," said Cora, her voice shaking with fear as the sharks swam into the cavern. They formed a sinister line in front of the mermaids and their dolphins.

"Look at their eyes—they're weird!" said Isla.

Cora realized she was right. The sharks' eyes were glowing a strange green color. Moving as one, they lowered their heads, their swordlike

noses pointing straight at them. Cora had never felt so scared in her life.

"Isla, use your magic!" screamed Maya.

"My bubbles can't fight them all," Isla cried.

"Cora! Use yours!" Sparkle called as the sharks started to swim toward them.

Cora saw the confusion on her friends' faces, but there was no time to explain. Isla's magic couldn't stop all the sharks—but maybe hers could! Imagining a gigantic whirlwave, she slapped her tail down hard.

The water in front of her instantly swirled into a funnel shape. She saw the sharks stop, confusion flickering across their faces. The whirlwave was big, reaching halfway up to the cavern roof, but Cora needed it to be much bigger!

"Hold my flipper, Cora! Let me help you," cried Sparkle. Grabbing hold, Cora felt energy whoosh into her from Sparkle, and her whirlwave suddenly shot up in size. Propelling it forward with her mind, she sent the spinning mass of water straight at the sharks!

Sparkle whistled in delight as the sharks turned tail and raced out of the cave. Cora sent the whirlwave chasing after them. As they reached the entrance, it caught them all up. They were whirled around in it and swept away across the reef.

"Cora? You have your magic!" Maya was delighted.

"Oh . . . my . . . wow!" breathed Amber in awe as they all watched from the tunnel.

"Cora, that was amazing!" cried Isla.

In the distance, the whirlwave exploded, sending the sharks flying in all directions. Cora realized there wasn't a moment to waste. Sharks could swim very quickly, and they could return at any minute. "We have to go," she said, swimming back into the cavern. Diving down, she picked up the two mini globes and tossed one to Amber. In two groups, they touched the globes and their dolphins.

"Mermaid Academy!" they shouted.

Once again, Cora had the sensation of the world vanishing around her. She was falling, falling . . . and then WHOOSH! She turned the right way up and saw that they were back in the Grand Cavern with green mermaid fire crackling on the wall.

"Oh, thank Neptune!" she gasped, relief washing over her. They were all safe—dolphins as well. The others clustered around her and Sparkle.

"Cora, you can make whirlwaves! That's awesome!" exclaimed Maya.

"When did you find your magic? Was it just after we'd left?" asked Isla.

Cora saw Sparkle's eyes silently begging her to tell the truth and made up her mind. She couldn't lie to her friends anymore. Not only was it making Sparkle unhappy, it was making her miserable too.

"Actually," she admitted, peeling off the seaweed bandage to reveal the outline of a silver whirlwave on her tail. "I discovered it yesterday."

"Yesterday?" Amber echoed.

"You found it and didn't tell us?" said Isla.

Cora saw the hurt on their faces and was immediately ashamed. "I'm sorry."

"I don't understand," said Maya in confusion. "Why did you keep it secret?"

Cora hesitated. She wasn't sure how to explain. Sparkle spoke up for her. "It was because of Issy. She seemed so sure she'd get her magic before Cora, and Cora didn't want to upset her."

"I'm sorry," Cora said in a rush. "I didn't want to lie to you, but Issy's used to doing things first. I didn't want to make her unhappy."

She saw understanding dawn in her friends' eyes.

"Well, I wish you had told us, but I get why you didn't," said Isla, squeezing her hand.

"It must be really hard with things like that when you're a twin," said Maya.

"You could have told us, though. We might not be twins, but we're your dorm-mates, and we're good at keeping secrets," said Amber.

Looking at the understanding on her friends' faces, Cora felt a rush of happiness. She was so lucky to be in Moon Pearl with them. "I won't ever lie to you again. Sparkle wanted me to tell the truth."

"Well, you should definitely listen to Sparkle in the future," said Isla with a smile.

Cora turned to Sparkle. "I will. I promise."

Sparkle kissed Cora's nose. "And I promise that I'll always speak up."

"Good," said Cora. "We should always tell each other the truth."

"Your tails!" Maya cried, pointing. "Look!"

Cora looked down. Sparkle's tail fin and hers had changed color, and they now had matching pink, dark-blue, and light-blue stripes.

"We've bonded!" she exclaimed, hugging Sparkle.

The dolphins whistled and clapped their flippers as Isla, Amber, and Maya whooped and cheered.

"Girls?" A sharp voice cut through the Grand Cavern. They swung around and saw Dr. Oceania frowning and swimming out of her study toward them. "What is going on?"

CHAPTER 11

Cora was gripped with panic as she saw the look on Dr. Oceania's face. They were going to be in real trouble for using the Magical Globe. Maybe they could pretend they had only just come into the cavern to look at it?

No, she thought firmly. *No more lies.*

"We used the Magical Globe to go to the Glass Ocean," she admitted. Dr. Oceania's frown deepened, but Cora continued: "We were trying to find out how the coral there was being damaged, and we asked the Sea Sphinx. She said we should go to the Glass Ocean at night. So we did, and we solved the mystery."

She explained about the sword sharks breaking through the coral and the gulper eels carrying it off. Then the other mermaids joined in, telling Dr. Oceania how the sharks' eyes had glowed green and how the sharks had teamed up to attack them. As Dr. Oceania listened, the stern look on her face was replaced by one of deep concern.

"It was almost as if someone was commanding them," said Isla.

"The Sea Sphinx did say they were servants," said Maya.

"Did any of you see anything else or feel anything strange?" Dr. Oceania asked quickly.

"Yes . . . ," said Cora. "It was just after I arrived there. My tail suddenly felt icy cold. And"—she took the silver disc shaped like a scale out of her bag—"I found this. I don't know what it is, but it

sure is strange." She handed it to Dr. Oceania.

Dr. Oceania's mouth tightened as she looked at it.

"We're so sorry, Dr. Oceania," said Isla. "We shouldn't have used the globe without asking, but we really wanted to try to find out how the reef was being damaged."

"And stop it," added Amber.

"Will we get behavior points?" asked Maya anxiously.

Dr. Oceania's face softened. "Not this time, girls. I think the scare you've had is punishment enough, and I do appreciate your desire to

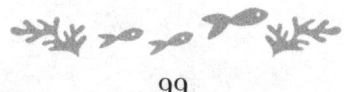

protect the coral reef. Those instincts will be helpful when you eventually become fully qualified guardians. I will organize guards to go there to stop the sharks and protect the reef from further damage. And I'm sure Ms. Rocksea will want your help repairing the coral in your next Coral Club session."

"Dr. Oceania?" said Isla, glancing at Cora. "If Cora wanted to swap to Coral Club from Medicine Club, would that be allowed?"

"I am sure that would be fine," said Dr. Oceania. She gave Cora a quizzical look. "If that's what you really want, Cora."

Cora was just about to nod when she hesitated. She loved being with her dorm-mates, but she was with them most of the time and she really wanted to learn how to play different musical instruments.

"I would like to change clubs," she said, meet-

ing Dr. Oceania's gaze. "But please may I do Music Club instead?"

She glanced quickly at her friends, wondering how they would react. To her relief, they all smiled and Maya gave her a big thumbs-up.

Dr. Oceania's eyes were warm. "Of course," she said to Cora. "That sounds like an excellent choice. I will let Ms. Melody know to expect you next Friday. Now, I think a hot drink and a snack would help you calm down before bedtime. Oh, and one last thing, girls. Can you please keep what happened tonight between yourselves? I don't want the other students talking about this and becoming worried."

They nodded and followed her to the dining room, where she gave them mugs of warm caramel sea foam and a large bag of urchinberry cookies to share.

While Dr. Oceania went to find some guards

for the reef, Moon Pearl headed back out to the Singing Circle. They sat on a stone bench, sipping their delicious drinks and sharing the cookies with the dolphins.

"That was an awesome adventure!" said Amber.

"It was scary!" said Maya.

"But really exciting," said Isla. "I'm glad we found out how the coral was being damaged so Dr. O can do something about it. But there are still a few mysteries we haven't solved yet, aren't there? Like, why were the sharks attacking the coral in the first place? And what were the gulper eels doing with it?"

"Also, why did the sharks work together?" said Maya. "Sword sharks don't usually do that."

"Sword sharks also don't usually have eyes that glow a weird green color," Amber pointed out.

"And what was that silver scale thing you found, Cora?" said Isla. "Dr. O was very interested in it, and the Sea Sphinx said we should *beware of bright scales*. It's all very fishy. Who else thinks we should try to find some more answers?"

"Me!" said Amber and Cora immediately.

"Me too, but no more breaking school rules," Maya begged.

"Okay," Isla agreed.

Amber grinned. "Not unless we really, really have to!"

They were interrupted by a shout from above them.

"Cora!" Cora looked up and saw Issy leaning out of her dorm window. She pointed at Cora's blue-and-pink-striped tail fin. "You've bonded with Sparkle!"

"Um . . . Yes," said Cora. "And . . ." She showed her the silver whirlwave at the top of her tail. "I found my magic too." Her tummy clenched anxiously. How would Issy react?

Issy beamed. "That's awesome!" She turned and called into her dorm. "Come look, everyone! Cora's found her magic!" She leaned back out. "What can you do, Cora?"

Cora felt a tidal wave of relief as she saw the genuine happiness on Issy's face.

"Why don't you show her?" Sparkle whispered.

Cora grinned and created a mini whirlwave. It swirled from her tail and rose, spinning into

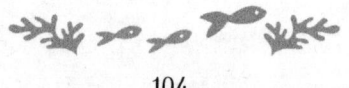

the air. It floated up until it was level with Issy's astonished face and then dissolved into a cloud of tiny bubbles, one of them popping on her nose.

Issy and her dorm burst out laughing and then clapped and cheered. Isla, Maya, and Amber joined in.

"That's so cool, Cor!" said Issy as the sound of the bedtime conch rang out. "Tomorrow morning, you'll have to tell me all about how you found your magic. Maybe it'll help me find mine!"

"Night!" Cora called as Issy waved and disappeared back into her dorm.

Cora sighed happily as she realized that for once, she didn't feel sad saying good night to Issy. She didn't want to be going to bed in any dorm except for Moon Pearl.

"Are you okay?" Sparkle asked, nudging her.

"More than okay," said Cora, kissing her nose. "Thank you."

"What for?" Sparkle asked.

"For helping me realize that it's all right for things to change, and that changes aren't always bad," said Cora.

"Changes like this, you mean?" said Sparkle, wiggling her tail fin.

Cora grinned and nodded, wiggling her matching tail back. "Exactly!" Bonding was one change she was very happy about!

Sparkle nuzzled her. "Some things change, but

others never do. I'll always be glad I asked to be your dolphin."

Cora took hold of her flippers and made a whirlwave that swirled above them. "And I'll always be glad I said yes!"

The whirlwave exploded, and she and Sparkle swung each other around as the cloud of sparkling bubbles floated down around them. Happiness rushed through Cora. Mermaid Academy was the only place in all the oceans where she wanted to be!

The mermaids are going on a field trip to study the wildlife! Can Maya help her dorm win the class prize for best project?

Read on for a peek at the next book in the Mermaid Academy series!

Mermaid Academy: *Maya and Rainbow* excerpt text copyright ©
2023 by Julie Sykes and Linda Chapman.
Cover art and excerpt illustrations copyright © 2023 by Lucy Truman.
Published by Random House Children's Books,
a division of Penguin Random House LLC,
1745 Broadway, New York, NY 10019.
Originally published in paperback in the United Kingdom
by Nosy Crow Ltd, London, in 2023.

Rainbow swam up to Maya and nudged her arm. "Maya, the others want us to play fin-ball!"

Maya looked up from her book and giggled. "Rainbow, you're tickling me!" She gave her dolphin a gentle push and spotted her friends from Moon Pearl dorm—Amber, Isla, and Cora—treading water a little way off with their dolphins, Flash, Bubble, and Sparkle.

"Come on," said Rainbow. "Let's go play." She wriggled her nose under Maya's arm. "Pleeeeease!"

Maya hesitated. Classes had finished for the

day, and the first-year students were relaxing in the Singing Circle. Maya had been hoping to read her new library book, *Bubble Tunnels for Beginners*. After that she planned to sketch the little nibbler fish that liked to chomp on the coral walls of Mermaid Academy.

"Get a swish on, Maya!" called Isla. "The boys from Sea Jet have challenged us to a rematch."

"This time we are definitely going to win!" said Amber.

Maya felt torn. Fin-ball was fun, but she really did want to finish her book before class tomorrow. Making bubble tunnels was a new topic, and Maya liked to get things right the first time, even if it meant putting extra work in. She'd been awarded two sea-star points by her teachers today for being prepared for her classes, and she hoped to get some more the next day. "You all go on without me," she said, her eyes already straying back to the page.

"No, Maya," protested Amber, swimming over. "We won't be as good a team without you."

"Pleeeeease come!" chorused Isla and Cora, joining her.

Rainbow swooshed her tail through Maya's hair, then used her nose to flip the book shut. She smiled at Maya. "Don't be a boring barnacle, Maya! Let's have some fun."

"I'm not a boring barnacle!" Maya protested. "I just want to make sure I'm ready for class tomorrow."

"You will be. You're always top of every class. Come on," Rainbow said. Slapping her flippers against her sides, she chanted, "Play! Play! Play!"

Maya gave in. Rainbow was a pretty pink dolphin who was patterned with bright rainbows. She loved having a good time, and Maya knew Rainbow wouldn't stop until she got her way.

"Okay, I'll keep reading after dinner," Maya said, slipping her book into her bag. As she got up, her tail tingled with excitement, and she realized she was really looking forward to the game. Since joining Mermaid Academy, she'd been practicing fin-ball whenever she had spare time, and now was a chance to test out her moves.

Her friends high-fived her. Rainbow did a

happy flip, then pushed her back fin into Maya's hand. "Let's go!"

Following her friends, Maya let Rainbow pull her through the sparkling turquoise water, her purple-blue-and-pink hair streaming out behind her. Moon Pearl dorm whooshed out of the Singing Circle, swimming between two of Mermaid Academy's majestic coral towers. Beyond the buildings, the school grounds stretched in all directions. Maya and her friends passed the playground with its awesome spinning clams and twisty mother-of-pearl slides, then glided through Tranquility Garden with its winding shell paths and beds of gently waving anemones.

"Who wants to race?" called Amber, smiling at her dolphin, Flash.

"Me!" shouted Isla and Bubble together, and the four of them sped ahead in a swirl of bubbles.

Maya and Cora grinned at each other as they

continued to swim along with their dolphins. Cora liked to look at wildlife as she swam, and Maya didn't want to race. She was content to chat with Cora and look at the creatures she pointed out.

Catching up with Isla and Amber at the fin-ball fields, they saw the merboys from Sea Jet dorm practicing their tail passes, flicking the sponge ball between themselves and their dolphins.

"We were starting to think you'd changed your minds about a rematch," said Obasi, catching the ball and spinning it on one finger.

"As if!" said Amber with a grin.

As they launched into the game, Maya quickly forgot about bubble tunnels. She charged up and down the field, ducking and diving their opponents. When she finally got the ball, she executed a perfect upside-down tail flick, smashing the sponge ball into their goal!

It was a fast and furious game. By the time the two teams gathered at the center for the last throw, it was three goals each. Nimesh got the ball, but Amber caught it during his pass and flicked it to Flash, who nosed it to Maya. Maya looked for Rainbow, but she was too far away, so Maya passed the ball to Isla. Bubble swam for the goal, and Isla flicked him the ball so he could hit it into the net.

"Yaaay! Four-three, us!" whooped Amber. "We win!"

UNICORN ACADEMY

MEET SOME UNICORN BEST FRIENDS IN THE BOOKS THAT INSPIRED THE NETFLIX SERIES!